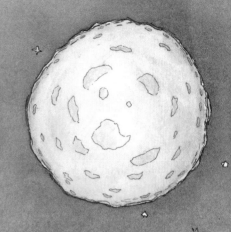

Wild Honey from the Moon

For Kaylan Adair,
editor extraordinaire

◇

First edition 2019

Library of Congress Catalog Card Number 2019939642
ISBN 978-0-7636-8169-2

19 20 21 22 23 24 CCP 10 9 8 7 6 5 4 3 2 1

Printed in Shenzhen, Guangdong, China

This book was typeset in Mrs. Eaves.
The illustrations were done in ink and watercolor.

Candlewick Press
99 Dover Street
Somerville, Massachusetts 02144

visit us at www.candlewick.com

Wild Honey from the Moon

KENNETH KRAEGEL

CANDLEWICK PRESS

Contents

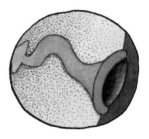

CHAPTER ONE

Hugo

On the last day of January, late in the evening, deep in the woods, a mother shrew worried about her sick young son.

She did not know what was wrong with her poor little Hugo. His feet were hot, his head was cold, and he just slept and slept.

She consulted Dr. Ponteluma's *Book of Medical Inquiry and Physiological Know-How*. Under the heading COLD HEAD, HOT FEET, SLEEPS A LOT, it read:

Unknown cause, very dangerous. One teaspoon of
wild honey from the moon has been known to cure.
"Oh, my!" Mother Shrew exclaimed.

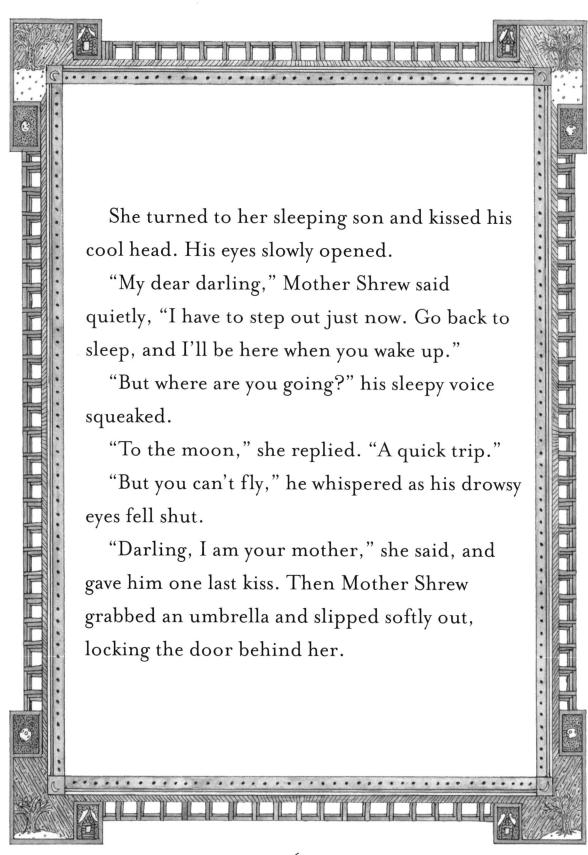

She turned to her sleeping son and kissed his
cool head. His eyes slowly opened.

"My dear darling," Mother Shrew said
quietly, "I have to step out just now. Go back to
sleep, and I'll be here when you wake up."

"But where are you going?" his sleepy voice
squeaked.

"To the moon," she replied. "A quick trip."

"But you can't fly," he whispered as his drowsy
eyes fell shut.

"Darling, I am your mother," she said, and
gave him one last kiss. Then Mother Shrew
grabbed an umbrella and slipped softly out,
locking the door behind her.

CHAPTER TWO

The Great Horned Owl

Mother Shrew climbed high into the treetops and stared up at the distant moon.

A cool voice broke into the quiet night.

"Why, hello, Mother Shrew," crooned the Great Horned Owl. "Shall I eat you now or save you for later?"

"My dear mortal enemy," Mother Shrew replied without taking her eyes off the moon, "you must eat me later, for right now I am on a mother's errand to the moon."

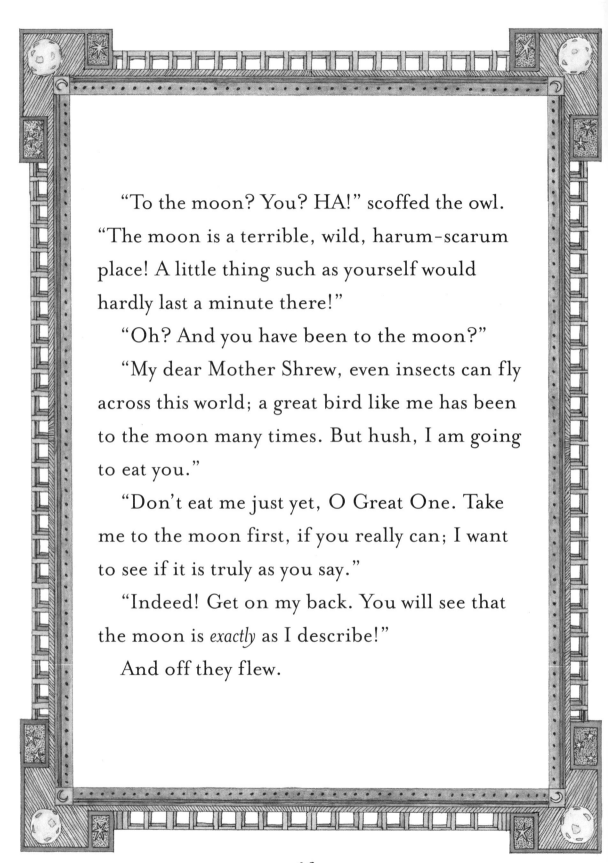

"To the moon? You? HA!" scoffed the owl. "The moon is a terrible, wild, harum-scarum place! A little thing such as yourself would hardly last a minute there!"

"Oh? And you have been to the moon?"

"My dear Mother Shrew, even insects can fly across this world; a great bird like me has been to the moon many times. But hush, I am going to eat you."

"Don't eat me just yet, O Great One. Take me to the moon first, if you really can; I want to see if it is truly as you say."

"Indeed! Get on my back. You will see that the moon is *exactly* as I describe!"

And off they flew.

As they drew near to the moon's surface, the owl said,
"So you see, Mother Shrew, I *can* fly to the moon. And
look! The night mares are stampeding! Yes, it is all as
dangerous as I said. Now, let us go back to our quiet
wood, where I will happily eat you after so long a flight."

"Some other time!" said Mother Shrew. "I must
get some wild honey for my dear little Hugo!" And
with that, she leaped off the wary owl and plummeted
toward the moon.

CHAPTER THREE

The Night Mares

Into the raging stampede Mother Shrew landed, managing to catch hold of a great bucking horse.

"There, there, dear," she soothed. "Let me sing you a song—it is my little Hugo's favorite."

As Mother Shrew sang, the horse slowly calmed to
a standstill.

"Now, then, mighty one, what is the problem?
Why do you all rage so?"

"Bad dreams, Mother. We are forever chased by
bad dreams."

Mother Shrew looked about. "Well, it is no
wonder, in a cold, gloomy place like this. Come,
let's see if we can find someplace sunny and warm.
That will do you good, and maybe, just maybe, I'll
find some honey for my Hugo, too!"

Mother Shrew directed the great horse toward a distant mountain range. After a long and difficult trek, they stood on a high peak looking down at the sunny side of the moon.

"Ah, that's better," Mother Shrew said with satisfaction.

As they descended the mountain, the mare slowed.
"It is . . . so warm . . . and *bright*!" Stumbling into the
soft grass, the weary horse was overtaken by sleep.

"Well, good-bye, then," whispered Mother Shrew.
"I must keep on. Sweet dreams, my friend!"

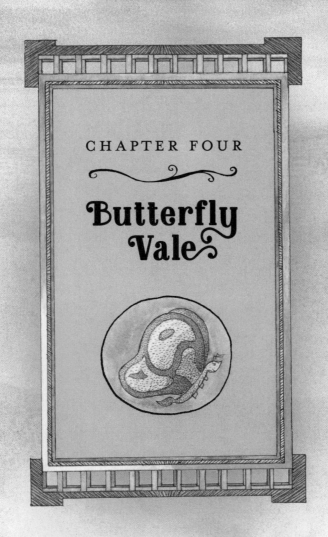

CHAPTER FOUR

Butterfly Vale

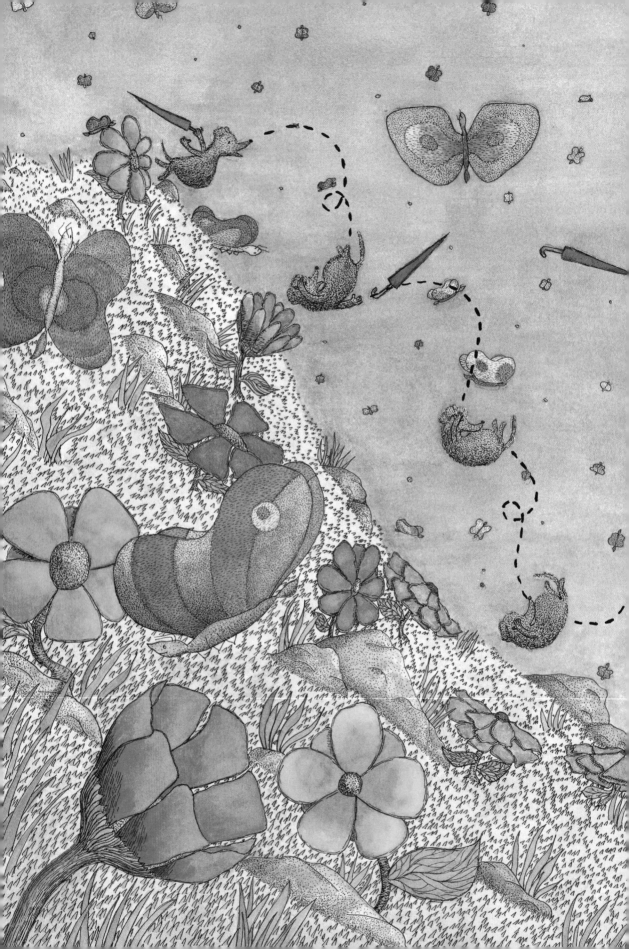

Mother Shrew plodded on, wondering how to find honey. She had been walking for some time when she rounded a corner and found herself on a high hill overlooking a wondrous valley.

"Oh!" Mother Shrew gasped. "It is so lovely!" She took a step closer, tripped, and rolled headlong down the hill.

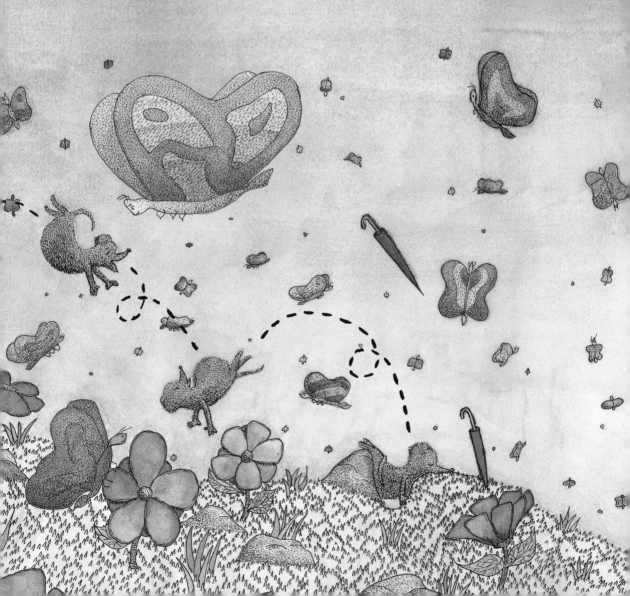

Six arms lifted Mother Shrew and gently laid her on something soft.

"Are you all right, Mother?" a thin, clear voice asked.

Glancing up, Mother Shrew found herself looking into the eyes of a great butterfly, glorious and fine.

"What a wonderful place! My head is spinning with the beauty of it!"

The butterfly smiled and handed her a cup. "Drink this, Mother."

A delicious sweet liquid ran down Mother Shrew's throat. It filled her with verve and vitality.

Mother Shrew sat straight up. "Honey? Is this wild honey from the moon?"

"No," the butterfly replied. "This is nectar. There is only one place on the moon where you will find honey."

"Oh," said Mother Shrew, disappointed. "Well, thank you for the nectar. I feel much better. But where is it that I can find honey?"

"On an island, in the garden of the Queen Bee," the butterfly said gravely. "But they will not treat you kindly there."

"I have no choice," Mother Shrew replied. "It is for my young son, Hugo, who is sick."

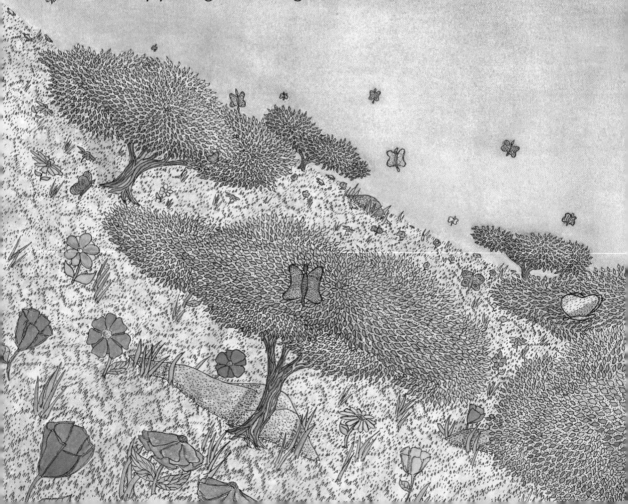

"I see." The butterfly paused in thought. "Well, if you are certain you must go, I can carry you there, Mother."

"Take me there, beautiful one."

With grace, the butterfly lifted Mother Shrew up and carried her over the sea.

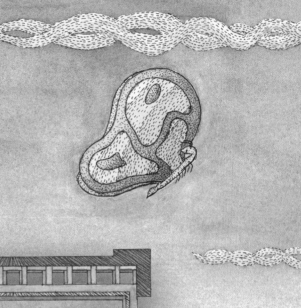

CHAPTER FIVE

The Garden of the Queen Bee

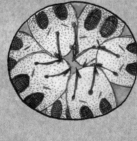

Mother Shrew pounded on the great door of
the garden with her umbrella. Instantly, she was shoved
back and surrounded by hundreds of angry bees.

"Hello," Mother Shrew began. "I have come to
request a teaspoon of honey for my ailing son."

"NO!" shouted a bee immediately, and another yelled
"NO!" and then another, and another.

"Very well," Mother Shrew said, "then I will ask the
quee—"

"NO!" they began all over again.

Mother Shrew frowned. "Really, I *must* see the queen."

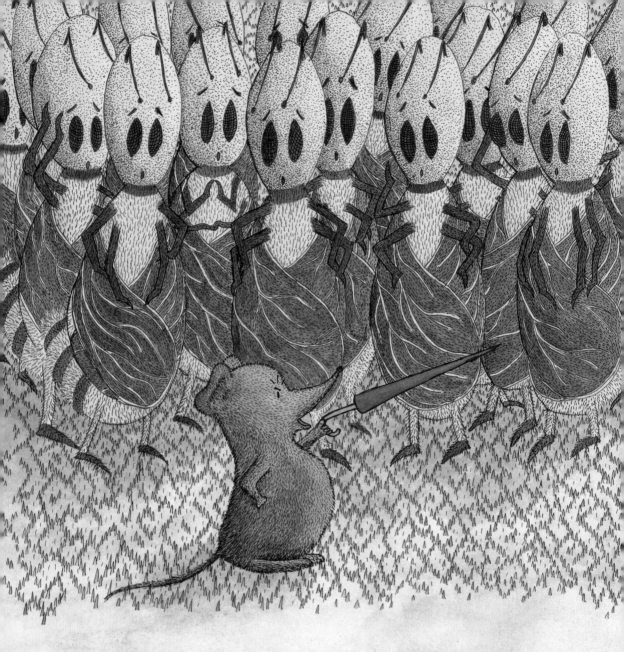

"SILENCE!" commanded Mother Shrew. A hush fell over the bees. "My dear sick son needs your honey to be well. So step aside. I am a mother on a mission, and I will *not* be held back!"

The bees stared at Mother Shrew for a moment and then obediently cleared a path for her.

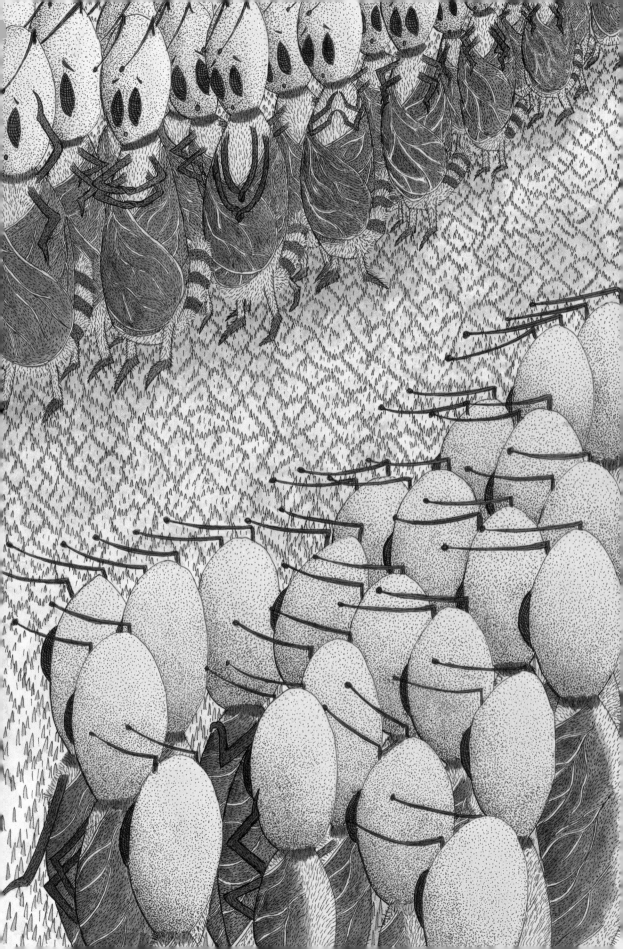

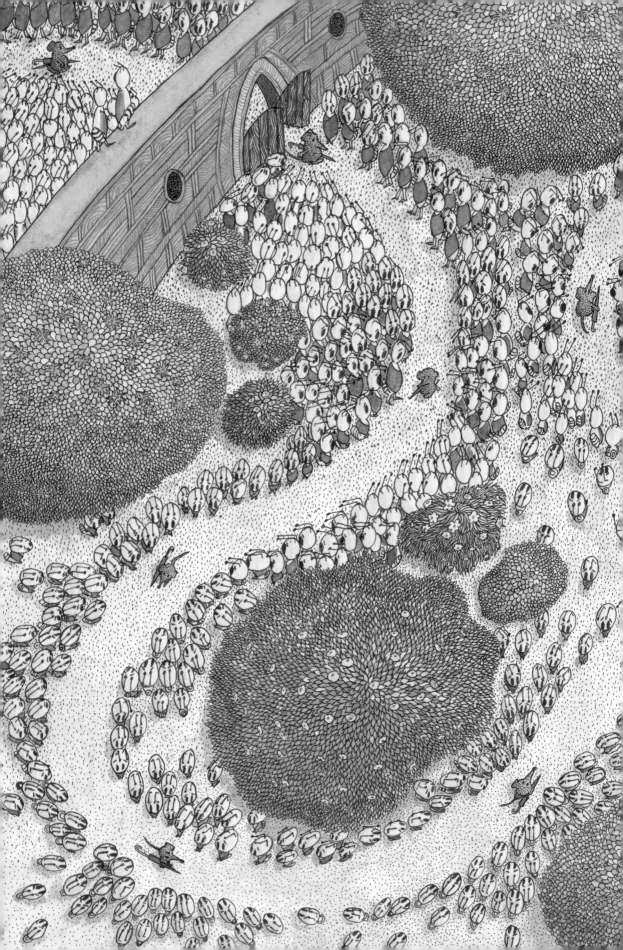

CHAPTER SIX

Wild Honey from the Moon

Mother Shrew stepped through the gate and into a lush, well-ordered garden, where the queen was waiting for her.

"Greetings, traveler," said the queen. "What brings you all the way here, into my garden?"

"Honey, Your Majesty," answered Mother Shrew. "I need some of your honey for my dear little Hugo, who is sick."

"Ah, I see! Then come with me, Mother Shrew. Come with me."

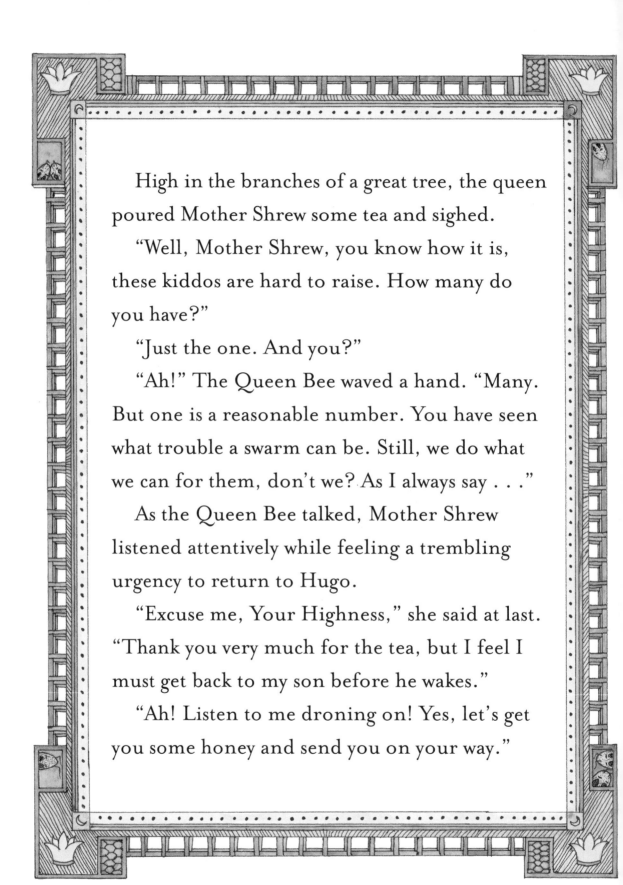

High in the branches of a great tree, the queen poured Mother Shrew some tea and sighed.

"Well, Mother Shrew, you know how it is, these kiddos are hard to raise. How many do you have?"

"Just the one. And you?"

"Ah!" The Queen Bee waved a hand. "Many. But one is a reasonable number. You have seen what trouble a swarm can be. Still, we do what we can for them, don't we? As I always say . . ."

As the Queen Bee talked, Mother Shrew listened attentively while feeling a trembling urgency to return to Hugo.

"Excuse me, Your Highness," she said at last. "Thank you very much for the tea, but I feel I must get back to my son before he wakes."

"Ah! Listen to me droning on! Yes, let's get you some honey and send you on your way."

The queen found a small jar of honey for Mother Shrew and walked her out of the garden. "Well, it has been a nice exchange of maternal feeling, hasn't it, Mother Shrew? I hope you will come again."

"I thank you kindly," Mother Shrew said, "and I do hope to visit again someday, but how do I get back home?"

"Oh! Hmmmm." The Queen Bee pondered the problem for a second. "Let's try this," she said, then took Mother Shrew's umbrella and plunged it hard into the surface of the moon. When she pulled it back out, a moonbeam shot out of the ground and down toward Earth.

"There you are, my lady. I wish you all the best!" With that, the Queen Bee ambled back into her garden.

CHAPTER SEVEN

The Return
of
Mother Shrew

Down, down, down, Mother Shrew glided through the night sky, holding the honey close. She had only just reached the treetops when a familiar cool voice again broke into the quiet of the night.

"Wellllllll, Mother Shrew, I did not expect to see you again!" The Great Horned Owl sneered. "Tell me how you liked the moon and then I will finally eat you."

"Eating, eating, eating," returned Mother Shrew. "You are always talking about eating this animal or that! Do you want to know what it is like to be eaten? Here, I'll show you!"

And Mother Shrew leaped up and bit the owl's ear until he shrieked and flew off, crying, "My ear! My ear!"

"Good riddance!" Mother Shrew muttered, and made her way home at last.

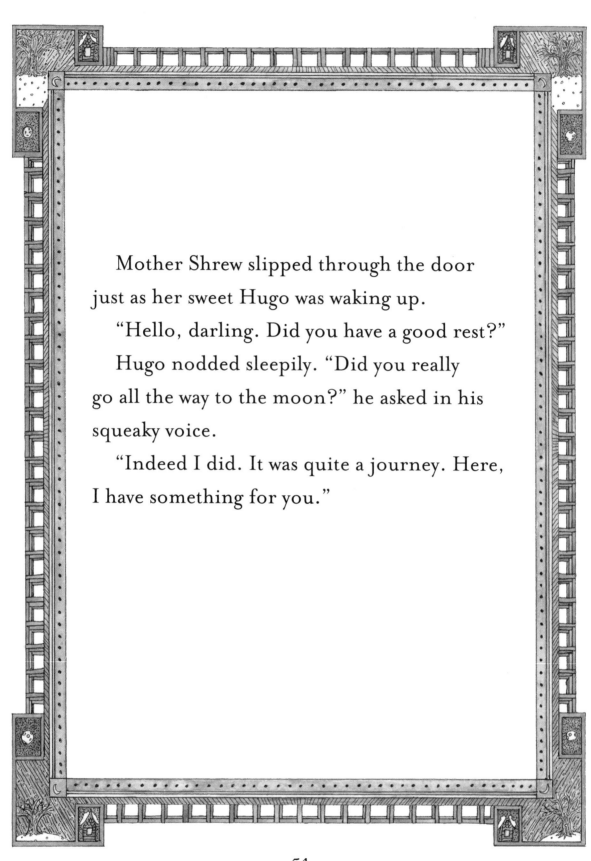

Mother Shrew slipped through the door
just as her sweet Hugo was waking up.

"Hello, darling. Did you have a good rest?"

Hugo nodded sleepily. "Did you really
go all the way to the moon?" he asked in his
squeaky voice.

"Indeed I did. It was quite a journey. Here,
I have something for you."

Mother Shrew dipped a spoon into her jar and
gave Hugo a taste of wild honey from the moon.

"Oh, my! That is good!" he exclaimed.

And to Mother Shrew's great delight, Hugo began
to feel better immediately.

And so, on the first day of February, early
in the morning, deep in the woods, a mother shrew
and her beloved son watched as the moonlight
slowly gave way to the warm light of dawn.